HURRICANE!

For Sally –
my saviour once again

ORCHARD BOOKS
96 Leonard Street, London EC2A 4XD
Orchard Books Australia
Unit 31/56 O'Riordan Street, Alexandria NSW 2015
First published in Great Britain in 2000
First paperback publication in 2001

A CIP catalogue record for this book is available
from the British Library.
1 86039 831 6 (hb)
1 84121 588 0 (pb)
1 3 5 7 9 10 8 6 4 2 (hb)
1 3 5 7 9 10 8 6 4 2 (pb)
Printed in Great Britain

TONY BRADMAN

HURRICANE!

ORCHARD BOOKS

One

Sean hurried along the main school corridor towards his sister's classroom, struggling against the tide of noisy kids heading the other way. He and Laura were supposed to meet at the end of every day so they could travel home together, and until last week, Sean had always waited for her to come to him.

But now he tried to make sure he got to *her* as soon as possible.

Sean reached Laura's classroom and glanced quickly through the open door. But the only person still in there was Laura's teacher, Miss Gordon, cleaning the whiteboard. Sean continued up the corridor, finally breaking into a run, making for the cloakroom at the end that the Year Fours used.

There was nobody else around in that part of the school, but even so, he nearly missed Laura at first. Then he heard sniffing, and saw her. She was sitting alone in a dark corner of the gloomy cloakroom, tucked behind a couple of PE bags hanging from the pegs. And she was crying softly.

'Oh, Laura,' said Sean, feeling that he'd let her down. 'I was as quick as I could be,

honest. Was it Tiffany and her mates again? Did they hurt you?'

'No... not really,' said Laura, looking up at him. Her short dark hair was all over the place, and her cheeks were wet with tears. 'They took my coat and bag and hid them, though,' she said, 'and I can't find them anywhere.'

'Never mind, Lol,' said Sean, gently. 'I'll find them for you.'

Lol was short for Lolly, the name Sean had given Laura on the day she was born. He had been barely two years old himself then, and unable to say 'Laura' properly. Sean's hair was fairer, but brother and sister had the same round face and brown eyes, and they had always been close. Which was just as well, thought Sean, considering what they'd had to put up with recently.

Six months ago they'd been happy, going to school in the part of London where they'd lived for as long as Sean could remember. Then over one of their special Sunday lunches, Mum and Dad had told them they were moving – and not to another street, but right out of London, to a place on the south coast. What's more, Mum and Dad planned to open a posh restaurant there.

Mum and Dad had often talked of 'escaping from the rat race', of course, and how they hated living in the city and loathed their jobs – Dad worked for a bank, Mum for a computer company. Sean also knew they liked to cook in their spare time, and had always dreamed of running their own business. But he had never imagined they would actually do something about it.

But they had. The family moved in

August, Sean and Laura had started at their new school in September, six weeks ago – and the problems had begun soon after that. Problems with money, problems with the house, problems with bullies; although Sean had only just found out that a gang of girls in Laura's class – Tiffany and her mates – was giving his sister a hard time.

Sean went back to the Year Six cloakroom to get his own coat and bag, then took Laura

out through the back entrance of the school building, and round behind the kitchens. He headed straight for the big wheelie bins, and scrambled up the side of the nearest one so he could peer over the top.

'But how did you know they'd put them in *there*?' said Laura, looking at him wide-eyed as he pulled out her bag and her navy-blue hooded coat, then jumped down. Luckily, neither coat nor bag had landed in anything mucky.

'I just know the way their tiny minds work,' sighed Sean, dusting her coat off and handing it back to her. At that moment, a sudden, sharp gust of wind whipped round the corner of the school building and blew hard against them. Sean could see it making Laura shiver despite her thick school sweatshirt. 'Come on then, Lol,' he said. 'We don't want to miss our bus, do we?'

They crossed the playground, all of the other kids having gone, most of them met by a parent or a minder, thought Sean, unlike him and his sister. Laura pulled on her coat and took her bag from Sean. She had stopped crying and dried her eyes, but Sean thought she still looked miserable. The bullying was really starting to get to her.

Laura was quiet and shy, which was probably why she was being picked on in the first place, Sean had realised. Not that she was a wimp. Sean knew she'd tried to stand up for herself, but that only seemed to have made matters worse. Tiffany and her gang obviously enjoyed a challenge, he thought. Sean decided then and there that he had to do something to help his sister.

But what? He couldn't protect her all the time. He had thought of telling a teacher, but getting one to believe him might be pretty tough. He didn't know any of the staff very well yet, and besides, from what Laura had said, Tiffany and her mates were the crafty sort – nasty little devils on the sly, perfect little angels when any teachers or big brothers were around.

No, there was only one thing for it, Sean decided as he and Laura went through the school gate and headed for the bus stop, the cold wind making him glad he was wearing his big black and yellow anorak. He'd have to tell Mum and Dad, although that was a problem in itself. They were so busy, and so wound up these days, they hardly seemed to take notice of Laura, or him.

'I'm going to check on Thumper as soon as we get home,' said Laura. The bus appeared at the corner. 'I think I might put him in the shed tonight...'

'Huh, you and that rabbit,' said Sean, distracted, not taking much notice as Laura chattered on about the pet she'd brought with her from London.

I have to make Mum and Dad listen, thought Sean...but will they?

Sean and Laura climbed on the bus, showed the driver their passes, and sat near the exit doors, about halfway along. None of the other kids seemed to go home by bus, and they were almost alone on it. The only other passenger was an old lady with a shopping trolley, and she got off at the next stop.

Laura talked about Thumper all through the ten-minute ride out of town and along the curving coast road. But Sean let her voice wash over him, concentrating on what he was going to say to Mum and Dad. He'd have to pick his moment, he thought, talk to them when they might actually *listen*.

The bus pulled up at their stop, fifty metres or so from their new house. Sean and Laura got off and were instantly buffeted by the wind, which had become much stronger and colder. It smelt of salt and ozone, and blew into their faces, pulling at their coats and spattering them with drops of seawater.

Sean had to admit they'd moved to a beautiful spot. On the right, wooded hills rose beside the road, and on the left stood a sea-wall, a couple of metres above a sandy beach. The sea was running higher than Sean had ever seen, with huge, green and glassy, white-capped waves crashing on to the sand. A mass of big black clouds filled the horizon, and was moving their way.

Directly ahead was the house – Mum and Dad's dream home. It was quite old, built of red brick and square, with a tiled roof, although that was being repaired and was mostly covered in blue plastic sheeting. The house stood on a bend where the road dipped down to the same level as the beach, the rear garden running alongside the sand, only a low fence between them.

A short drive led from the road to the front of the house, and as usual it was blocked by their old estate car, a builder's van, and a skip, as well as heaps of bricks, bags of cement, and piles of timber. There was a sign on the house that said *The Smugglers' Inn*,

and beneath it the front door was wide open. But Sean and Laura went down the narrow side passage instead.

They emerged in the rear garden, which was much larger than the tiny patch of weeds they'd had in London. This garden was mostly lawn, with an old wooden shed at the far end, Thumper's new hutch and run

standing to one side of it. Behind the shed and the hutch was a high fence marking the end of their property. And directly behind that stood three tall ash trees in a line, hiding the garden from the road that rose steeply along the edge of the cliff beyond, their branches tossing as they bore the brunt of the wind.

'Will you take my bag in for me, Sean?' Laura asked, holding it out to him, her face eager, more like the old Laura. 'I'll only be a few minutes.'

'Sure,' said Sean, hefting her bag on to his other shoulder and watching her run up the garden. It was probably best if he spoke to Mum and Dad on his own first, he thought. He went in the back door – and straight into chaos.

Sean had come into what was supposed to be the restaurant's kitchen. This morning it had been the usual mess, the recently delivered ovens and burners still not fitted yet, pipes and wires hanging from the replastered walls. But now one of those walls – on the beach side of the house – had a large hole in it, and the room seemed filled with wind and noise and dust.

'Hey, Sean, how you doin', son?' shouted Ray, the burly, bearded chief builder, switching off the big drill he was holding. He spoke in the slight local accent Sean still couldn't quite get used to, but he was friendly and funny, as were his mates Steve and Eddie, who both smiled and nodded hello. 'Your mum and dad are upstairs,' said Ray, starting his drill again.

'Thanks,' shouted Sean. He left the kitchen and went into a larger room, the one that would eventually be the main part of the restaurant, covering almost the entire ground floor of the house. The plan was for Sean and Laura and their mum and dad to live on the floor above, which had plenty of space.

And all of it in almost as much of a mess as the kitchen, thought Sean as he trudged up the uncarpeted stairs. He could hear the low murmur of the TV coming from the bedroom they were using as the lounge, and opened the door. Mum and Dad were sitting on the sofa, deeply engrossed in some bills.

'Oh, hi, Sean,' said Mum, smiling briefly at him. She was wearing old jeans and a jumper, her thick blonde hair tied back in a ponytail. 'You'll have to make your own tea, I'm afraid. There's a problem with the ventilation for one of the ovens, so we're, er...having a bit of a crisis.'

'You can say that again,' Dad muttered, then glanced up. He was wearing jeans too, and a faded sweatshirt, and his dark, wavy hair was covered with dust. 'You'd better make Laura something while you're at it,' Dad said.

'OK,' said Sean, thinking that he always did anyway, dumping Laura's bag in the corner along with his own. Then he turned back to Mum and Dad. 'Actually, I, er... wanted to talk to you about Laura,' he said, 'she's been...'

'Not now, Sean,' Dad groaned impatiently, cutting him off. 'Look, we just don't have time to sort out arguments between you kids. We'll talk to you later, but at the moment we've got more important things on our plate, OK?'

Sean frowned and opened his mouth to reply, but Mum spoke first.

'Sssh!' she hissed, suddenly. 'Quick, Phil, turn up the TV,' she said.

Dad grabbed the remote and did as he was told. All three of them turned to look at the screen, which showed a newsreader from the local station.

'*...I repeat*,' she was saying, a serious expression on her face, '*The Met Office has just issued an extreme weather warning for the south coast...*'

WEAT ER

Three

Sean could sense his mum and dad growing more tense as they listened. A weatherman took over from the newsreader to fill in the details, pointing on his map to a long, spiky line that was obviously threatening the coast. Sean realised it represented those black clouds he'd seen on the way home.

A big storm – a *very* big storm – was heading in their direction.

'We're expecting hurricane force winds later on,' said the weatherman, the map changing to a satellite picture, 'and they could cause structural damage. So batten down the hatches, folks, it looks like we're in for a pretty stormy night. And now it's back to *Looking Good in the Garden...*'

The screen changed, and just then an extra-powerful gust of wind seemed to slap the side of the house, making the window rattle and drowning out the theme tune of Mum's favourite programme. Sean heard the plastic sheeting on the roof flapping hard, and saw Mum and Dad exchange nervous glances.

'We'd better have a word with Ray about, er...battening down those hatches,' said Dad, standing up and heading for the door, Mum following him.

'You did send that cheque in for the insurance, didn't you?' she said.

'Of course I did,' said Dad. 'I'm sure we're covered for storm damage.'

'Hang on a second,' said Sean, trying to get their attention. 'Laura—'

'You heard your dad, Sean,' said Mum, turning to him and looking cross. 'I'm sorry, but you don't seem to realise – this could be a real emergency.'

Then Mum and Dad were gone, leaving Sean alone with his thoughts. He went to the window. The clouds were closer, the light fading from the late October sky, the sea wilder than ever. He felt cross himself. He and Laura *never* argued with each other, and *of course* he realised this could be a real emergency. But as far as Mum and Dad were concerned, everything seemed to be an emergency these days. Except when it came to their children, that is.

Sean found himself wondering uneasily if he and Laura mattered to his mum and dad at all any more. It was as if the house and the restaurant came first, last and in between. Oh sure, he thought, Mum and Dad *said* they were doing it to give Sean and Laura a better future, not just themselves. Sean was worried about the present, though, and what Laura was having to go through every day. Then he heard the door open behind him, and Laura come in.

'What's up with Mum and Dad now?' she said, sitting on the sofa without taking off her coat, shoulders hunched, hands deep in her pockets, her face glum again.

'I passed them on the stairs, and they barely said hello.'

'I'm sure they didn't mean anything by it,' said Sean, not wanting her to be upset. 'They're...just worried about the weather. I'll make us some tea.'

'Thanks, Sean,' said Laura. 'If it wasn't for you and Thumper, I'd...'

'Forget it, Lol,' said Sean, feeling he didn't deserve any gratitude, not until he'd got Mum and Dad to listen, at least. If they ever did, that is.

Sean went into the small bedroom they were using as a temporary kitchen, put some sliced bread in the toaster on the floor, took two box drinks from off the top of the microwave, and listened to the rain beating against the window. He was glad he hadn't taken his coat off, either. The house was

absolutely freezing, the wind seeming to get into every nook and cranny.

He took the toast and the drinks to Laura, and they huddled together to watch TV, the weather growing steadily worse. Sean felt restless. Mum and Dad hadn't always been

like this, he brooded. Before the move they'd been pretty nice as parents go, and the four of them had got along. Surely they would help Laura if they knew what was happening to her, he thought...

Sean decided to have one more try, and

went downstairs. Mum and Dad were talking to Ray in the kitchen, and Sean went straight up to them.

'Mum, Dad,' he said. The adults fell silent and turned to him. 'Maybe this *isn't* the right time,' said Sean, 'but I do need to talk to you about Laura. We haven't been arguing, she just isn't very happy, and that's because—'

'Well we've got some news that might make her more cheerful,' said Dad, brightly, Ray smiling as well. 'It's probably not going to be all that comfortable here tonight with the storm coming—' Dad continued.

'So Ray's very kindly offered to put you and your sister up,' said Mum. 'It's Saturday tomorrow, and you don't have to go to school. We'll come and collect you in the morning, OK? I'll pack a bag for the both of you.'

Mum said they'd be fine, that Ray and his wife were smashing people and had three kids themselves, so maybe Sean and Laura could make some friends. Meanwhile Mum and Dad would stay behind to look after the house.

It sounded sensible the way Mum said it, thought Sean – but he wasn't convinced. In fact, he was angry now. He felt he and his sister were being dumped so Mum and Dad could focus on what they cared about most...their precious house and restaurant. But what about Laura – and what about *him*? Shouldn't they be more important to their parents than anything else?

Soon Sean was sitting sullenly in Ray's van, Laura between him and Ray, Mum and Dad together in the drive under a big umbrella. Laura waved to them as Ray turned the ignition key. Sean didn't, refusing even to look.

'It's not far, just over the hill,' said Ray, switching on the van's wipers and lights. It was rapidly getting dark, the rain hammering down. 'And you must know at least one of my kids, Laura. Isn't Tiffany in your class?'

Laura stiffened beside Sean, and gripped his hand tightly.

They turned into the bend behind the house, then took a right past a small electricity substation set in the trees. Power cables looped from it to a pylon up the hill, which stood before a field with an old caravan in one corner, the village starting just beyond. Steve and Eddie were in the back of the van, and Ray dropped them off before pulling into the drive of his cottage.

Ray got out of the van with Sean and Laura, and they dashed through the rain to the porch. Ray opened the door and they went inside; Sean was nervous, wondering if the rest of Tiffany's family might be the same as her. Perhaps Ray's friendliness was an act, he thought, perhaps Ray was an ogre and his wife a witch, and they would treat him and Laura like Hansel and Gretel...

But Ray's wife turned out to be nice – a big, red-haired woman who fussed over them, gave them a hot meal and showed them where they'd be sleeping. Ray had phoned ahead on his mobile, and Mrs Ray (as Sean thought of her) had made up two camp-beds for them in a little back room on the ground floor. Sean put their bag on a chair, and he and Laura took their coats off.

'You should be cosy in here whatever the weather's doing,' said Mrs Ray, pulling the curtains across the french doors that led into the garden. Sean caught a glimpse of spooky-looking bushes thrashing madly in the storm, their leaves briefly silvered by moonlight, and he heard the wind booming.

'Blimey, listen to that,' said Ray. 'It's definitely not a night to be outside, is it? Come on, you two, I think there's a good film on TV this evening.'

It *was* a good film, one Sean wanted to see. Ray was as friendly as ever, and it was almost pleasant sitting in the front room, enjoying the movie with Mrs Ray, Robbie, their red-haired six-year-old, and Madison, the dummy-sucking toddler curled up on her dad's lap. But Tiffany was there as well, stretched on the floor in front of the TV; Laura was lying there too, keeping herself at arm's length, her whole body looking stiff and uncomfortable.

Tiffany had been all sweetness and light when they'd arrived, a blonde, blue-eyed, smiling angel, although Sean could tell she was worried he and Laura might reveal what she'd been up to at school. But Sean knew Laura wouldn't say a word, and he wasn't going to tell Ray and Mrs Ray, who both obviously thought Tiffany was wonderful. Sean could see that being near Tiffany made Laura unhappy, but there wasn't much he could do about it, he decided, beginning to feel fed up with worrying and looking out for his sister.

'Actually, I've been thinking Laura might prefer to sleep in Tiff's room,' said Mrs Ray when the film ended. 'You'd like that, girls, wouldn't you?'

'Of course we would, Mum,' said Tiffany, smiling sweetly. Laura glanced at Sean, her eyes pleading desperately. Sean almost said something to Mrs Ray, but then decided he didn't want the hassle, and kept quiet instead.

Not long after that, Mrs Ray put Robbie and the sleeping Madison to bed upstairs, while Ray transferred one of the camp-beds to Tiffany's room. He also told Sean and Laura they could call their mum and dad if they wanted.

'Sean, you've got to do something,' Laura hissed in Sean's ear when they were alone. He punched out their home number on the buttons of the phone in the hall. 'I don't want to spend the night in *her* room. I can't, I *won't*—'

'Well, you've got to,' Sean hissed back, hearing the unavailable signal. 'What am I supposed to do? Tell Ray and his wife you don't want to sleep in their daughter's room because she's a nasty little bully? Give me a break, Lol. They wouldn't believe it. Anyway, she's not going to kill you, is she?'

Sean tried the number again, ignoring Laura as she walked off into the back room. He still couldn't get through, either to the main phone, or to Mum or Dad's mobiles, but that was no surprise, as Mum and Dad never remembered to keep them charged. Sean put the phone down at last, told himself he wasn't really bothered, and went to watch some more TV.

But he *was* bothered. Tiffany was watching TV too, and gave him a very smug look that said she knew he wouldn't grass on her. But Sean was more concerned about why the phone at home wasn't working, whether it could have anything to do with the storm. Then he realised the wind outside was blowing harder than ever. It was roaring now, almost beating at the cottage.

'We interrupt this programme to bring you the latest update on the coastal storm,' said a voice on the TV, breaking into Sean's thoughts. He looked at the screen and saw the same weatherman from earlier. 'Well, folks, global warming certainly seems to be pushing our weather to extremes. This storm is a real humdinger, and we've been getting some very disturbing reports...'

Sean listened with mounting anxiety. 'Ships blown ashore...damage to buildings... phone lines down.' Tiffany changed channel, but suddenly Sean wanted to find Laura, regretting the way he'd spoken to her, wondering uneasily what she was doing. He went into the hall, and stopped, noticing the back room door was ajar. A freezing draft was whistling through the gap.

Sean pushed the door open, stepped into the room and shut the door behind him. The main light was on, and the french windows were wide open to the night, the curtains whipped by the wind, rain spattering on the edge of the carpet.

Laura wasn't in the room, and her coat wasn't where she'd left it, on a chair with Sean's, either. Sean's heart seemed to lurch, and he felt a terrible fear rising in him – Laura must have run away, he thought, into the storm.

Sean grabbed his coat, pulled it on – and he ran out into the storm, too.

Sean had one thought in his mind, and one thought alone – he *had* to find his sister and save her from the dangers of this storm. But it was only when he stepped outside the cottage that he realised how violent the weather had become in the last few hours. The wind instantly caught him in the back, sending him staggering across Ray's patio and crashing into a fence.

It was a tall fence, like the one behind the shed in Sean's garden, and for a few seconds the wind pressed him against it, his face grinding into the rough wood. Then he managed to turn his head, saw he was near the end of the narrow side passage to Ray's cottage, and moved that way, pulling himself along the fence, feeling it tremble and sway as the wind battered it.

The passage sheltered him from most of the wind, but the wooden door at the other end was banging backwards and forwards, and Sean made for it, hoping Laura was just beyond. But she wasn't. Sean stepped out on to the cottage's drive, into the wind and rain again, and edged past Ray's van, finally arriving at the gateway they'd driven through a few hours before.

There were flashes of moonlight now, and

Sean looked down the road, then up it, the wind sweeping over and round him, booming and whistling in his ears, tossing the branches of the trees in the gardens opposite. The air was full of rain and leaves and bits of rubbish too, and then a big plastic dustbin suddenly tumbled past, bouncing and clattering, its lid long gone.

And there was absolutely no sign of Laura, not in any direction.

Sean stood there hesitating, thinking hard, the wind scouring at his face and flattening his anorak against his body. What was Laura thinking? She didn't want to spend the night in Tiffany's room, so she had run away. But Sean knew Laura wasn't stupid, and would certainly make for home. She only had a few minutes start on him, so he *must* be able to catch up with her.

Sean took a couple of steps, but paused and looked back at the cottage, thinking he should tell Ray, maybe ask Ray to go after Laura in the van...although that would definitely mean having to explain about Tiffany. No, it would be better if he just got on with it himself, Sean thought, and he set off again, leaning into the wind, eyes narrowed, chin pressed down on his chest.

When Ray had driven them here earlier, Sean hadn't taken much notice of what lay on either side of the road. Now he saw the village petered out after only a few more houses. The field with the caravan in the corner lay beyond them, the woods beginning at the field's far edge, the pylon standing taller than the trees, its metal gleaming for a moment in a flash of moonlight.

At least the rain seemed to be easing a

little, Sean thought, and glanced up at the sky...just in time to see the moon swallowed again by a huge, dark cloud, the world instantly plunging into blackness. Then the rain and the wind seemed suddenly to double in force, driving into him, snatching his breath away, making his heart race and his throat tighten with anxiety.

Sean lowered his head into the wind, struggling to stay on his feet...then he heard a strange bumping noise. He looked up, startled, and at that moment the cloud passed and the moon lit the world in its silver glow again. Ahead of him was a low hedge, with the old caravan just beyond it. And that's where the noise was coming from – the caravan was rocking in the wind.

Suddenly it started to roll over, crushing the hedge, teetering there for a second...

then finally tipping upside down on to the road with an almighty *CRASH!*, collapsing in on itself, its windows exploding outwards. Sean ducked, protecting his face with his arms, feeling a shower of glass and metal spatter like hail against his sleeves, the front of his coat and trousers.

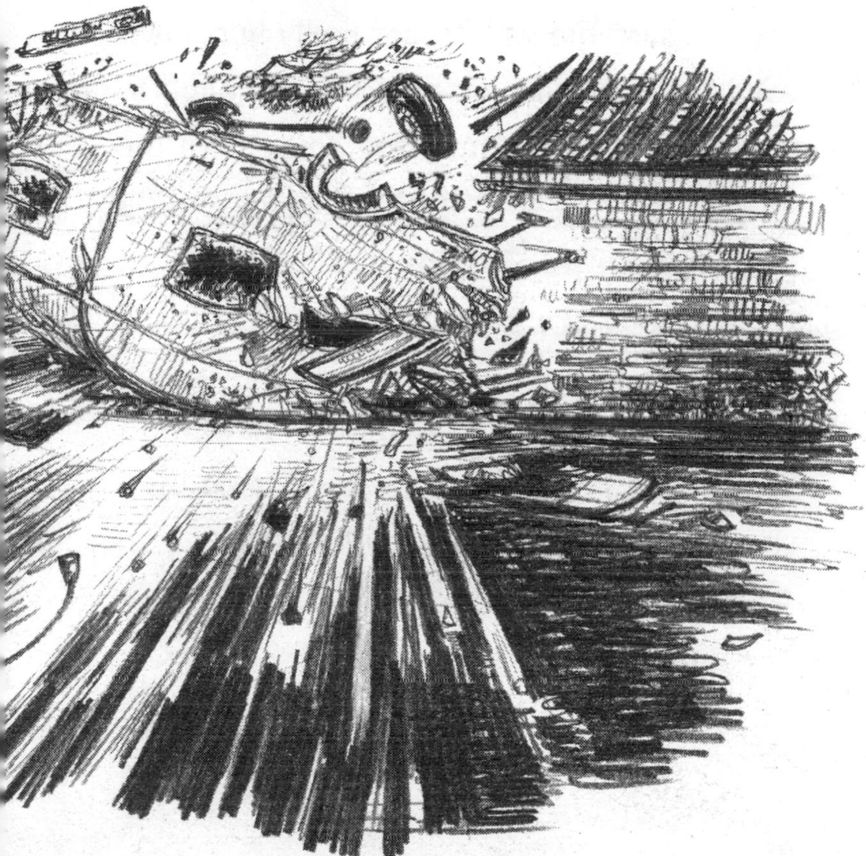

But the wind hadn't finished with the caravan, and pushed it along the road with a screeching sound of tearing metal. Sean hurriedly scampered out of its way, staring amazed as it hit the wall of somebody's garage head on, that end totally crumpling under the impact, a wheel flying off. Sean watched the wheel bounce a couple of times, then thump into a parked car.

Sean nearly turned and ran then, back to the safety of Ray's house, aware that being exposed to the kind of storm that could blow a caravan out of a field and along a road was crazy, a sure-fire way to get badly hurt or even killed. Nobody else was mad enough to come out, not even from the house with the garage that had been hit by the caravan. But Laura was in this storm somewhere, Sean thought guiltily – and all because *he* had let her down.

So it was his job to find her – however dangerous that might be. Sean squared his shoulders, took several deep breaths, struggled to get his pounding, frightened heart under control, then fought onwards.

'Please...please, God, don't let anything happen to Laura,' he prayed quietly as he continued up the hill, the wind grabbing the words and tossing them away. But it helped stop him thinking about how spooky the woods looked in the flickering moonlight, the clouds now rags and tatters blown across the sky, the rain reduced to drops and sprays swept from the trees.

It was like a night scene from a horror film with vampires and monsters, Sean thought as he crested the hill and started down the other side, or a scary fairy tale, a story to give you nightmares. And then he glimpsed somebody in the distance – somebody who looked exactly like a character from a fairy tale, a small, hooded figure running ahead of him, making for the main road.

Sean put on a spurt, sure it was Laura. He shouted her name over and over even though he knew she couldn't possibly hear him above the sound of the storm. He quickly gained ground on her, and became aware that the main road was shrouded in a strange white mist that seemed to leap every so often, the moonlight giving it a silvery radiance...then Laura ran into it, and vanished.

It was a spooky moment, and Sean stopped in his tracks. A sharp *CRACK!* made him jump and whirl round. He saw a wire fence with big, grey steel cabinets behind it, and huge coils with cables running upwards from them, and realised he'd come as far as the electricity substation. Then he caught sight of movement beyond it, shadows on shadows, something falling...

A huge tree *SMACKED!* down on to the substation with a terrifying noise, snapping the power cables with a distinct *TWANG!*, one of them swinging in a hissing arc through the air, blue sparks showering from its severed end.

Sean stood rooted to the spot, watching death come straight towards him.

Six

The cable swooshed past, centimetres above Sean's head, sparks cascading on to the road around him, an acrid, burning smell filling the air. Sean heard the cable slap down not far behind him, and instinctively hunched his shoulders. Then he turned round, slowly. The cable was slithering and coiling on the wet

Tarmac a few metres away, like a long thin snake spitting blue fire.

Crackles, buzzes and popping sounds were coming from the substation, and suddenly a sheet of orange flame whooshed up from beneath the fallen tree, the pulse of searing heat it gave off bringing Sean back to his senses. He looked round, saw the sub-station engulfed in fire, and took to his heels, the orange glare behind giving him a leaping, jerking shadow as he ran.

Sean soon arrived at the point where Laura had vanished, and he plunged into the strange white mist himself, the sting of salt on his lips telling him instantly it was sea spray. He turned left on to the main road, slipping and falling as he did so, scrambling quickly to his feet, scared he might get run over, and found himself beyond the mist, an incredible view before him.

The sky was clear of cloud now, the moon riding high and illuminating the coast as far as the town, although no lights seemed to be showing there. Sean wondered if that might have anything to do with what he'd just seen happening at the substation. The road was empty, not a single car or bus in sight, its surface slick with water and gleaming silver in the moonlight.

But it was the sea that really made Sean goggle. Enormous, relentless waves were rolling in at a steep angle to the beach, the wind whipping at their white-capped tops and driving massive walls of water into the cliff behind the house. Spray shot upwards in giant explosions when the water hit the rock, then turned into a swirling mist as it descended over the road.

The house itself looked tiny against the sea, almost like a doll's house, thought Sean, although at least it still seemed to be in one piece. He was relieved to see that the roof was on under its plastic sheeting, and guessed the trees at the end of the garden must be providing some shelter from the force of the wind and the waves. But there was no sign of Laura anywhere.

Sean's fear for his sister deepened and merged with his fear for himself. An image popped into his mind – like a flashback in a horror movie – of that broken cable swinging towards him. If it had been a little lower, he found himself thinking... and he suddenly felt sick. Then he realised one of his hands was hurting badly from where he'd fallen, and he started to shiver.

He ran on, desperate to get to the house,

deciding Laura must already have reached it and gone inside, and pushed into a dark corner of his mind any idea she might have got lost, or hurt, or worse... Sean ran faster and faster, his legs almost collapsing beneath him, his breath coming in gasps. He made it at last to the drive, passing the car and the skip, the wind beating at him...

He reached the front door, and pounded frantically on it.

'Mum! Dad!' he yelled at the top of his voice. *'LET...ME...IN!'*

There was no answer, so Sean moved to the side to peer through one of the downstairs windows. It was dark in the house, but then he saw a beam of light probing in the gloom, and realised somebody was using a torch to find their way to the front door. Sean moved back to it, and was about to start pounding again when he heard a ripping noise coming from above him.

He glanced upwards and saw that the plastic sheeting on the roof had almost been torn off. It was flapping and snapping wildly; like a sail being stripped from a mast, Sean thought, the wind trying to snatch it, pulling at the ropes still holding it to the gutter that ran round beneath the tiles. And as he watched, the sheeting finally ripped free and

flew off into the night sky.

It was immediately followed by a couple of roof tiles, their small, dark, ridged shapes spinning down, one hitting the edge of the skip and exploding into pieces, the other just missing the car bonnet and thumping into a flower bed beyond. Sean flattened himself against the front door, then felt it open behind him. He turned round, and was dazzled by a beam of torchlight.

'Sean! What the hell...' yelled a voice. It was Dad, shouting to be heard over the sound of the wind. 'What are you doing here? I can't believe you've made Ray bring you all the way back in this hurricane.' Dad glanced crossly beyond Sean. 'I'd better go and have a word with him, apologise...'

'Ray didn't bring me back, Dad,' yelled Sean, holding his hand in front of his eyes, unable to see his father's face properly. 'I... I came on my own.'

'You did *what*?' shouted Dad, horrified. 'I don't understand...'

'Get him inside, Phil, for heaven's sake!' yelled Mum, pushing past Dad to haul Sean in, slamming the door. 'Just look at the state of his coat!' she said, shining her torch at a big rip in his sleeve. 'And he's soaked through, too!'

'Is Laura here?' said Sean, unable to hold the question in any longer.

'No, she isn't,' said Mum, fear creeping into her face now; the three of them standing in the wavering torchlight, the wind howling outside.

'She should be at Ray's, and so should you,' said Dad, frowning. 'You've got some explaining to do, my lad. Have you two been arguing again?'

'No, we haven't,' snapped Sean angrily, his feelings suddenly boiling up inside him, his eyes prickling with tears. 'We *never* argue,' he shouted, 'but you've forgotten that because you're obsessed with the house and restaurant, and you just don't care about us any more, and if Laura gets killed it will be *YOUR* fault, not mine.'

'What on earth are you talking about,

Sean?' said Mum. She grabbed him hard by his shoulders, her torch digging into his left arm. 'Why do you think Laura might get killed?' she asked, staring intently at him, her voice rising with panic. 'Did something happen up at Ray's?' she yelled. 'Tell us!'

'OK!' Sean yelled back. 'I was trying to tell you earlier, but you wouldn't listen. Laura's being bullied at school by a girl called Tiffany, and when we got to Ray's house tonight we found out Tiffany is his daughter. Laura was upset and she wanted me to do something, but I didn't...and she ran away.'

'Oh, my God,' said Dad. 'You mean she's out in this storm somewhere?'

'But why didn't you stop her, Sean?' said Mum, letting him go, her face confused, trying to take in what he'd said. 'You must have realised...'

Sean wanted to scream at his mother, tell her he'd never imagined Laura would put herself in danger, but a terrific noise made them all look upwards.

The wind was wrenching the roof from the house.

Seven

Sean could hear what sounded like wood straining and grinding and cracking above them, and the wild howling of the wind outside reaching a crescendo. Dad opened the front door, and the wind rushed past him into the house like an invisible creature nosing furiously into every space. Dad peered

round the door, and Sean looked out into the night too, Mum behind them both.

Then there was a loud *SNAP!* and *CRUNCH!* overhead, and Sean knew the roof was going even before he saw a large, dark shape fall across the sky and land on the drive with a huge *THUMP!*, obliterating the car, the shock wave pushing them back harder than the

wind, tiles shattering into fragments that whacked into the house like shrapnel, smashing all the front windows.

Sean cried out in fright as a fragment hit the doorframe, splintering into smaller pieces that flew past his head, making him duck, his hands over his face. Mum screamed at Dad to shut the door, and pulled Sean deeper into the house, dragging him through the ground floor to the bottom of the stairs, where she stopped. Dad got the door closed, and followed them.

'Sweet Jesus, did you *see* that?' yelled Dad, looking anxiously up the stairs as if he expected the whole top floor to be torn off next. He turned to Sean. Mum was shining her torch on to Sean's face, holding his chin, examining his head for damage. 'Is he OK, Debbie?' said Dad.

'I'm absolutely fine,' snapped Sean, angrily freeing himself from Mum's grip and moving back from both his parents. 'Anyway, what do either of you two care? I'm not made of bricks and you won't be able to make money out of me. I'm just one of your children, so I don't really matter, do I?'

'Of *course* you do!' shouted Mum, her

voice cracking. Sean suddenly realised she was nearly in tears. 'I know we've been busy with the move and the house and everything,' she said, 'and maybe we haven't paid as much attention to you as we should. But you and Laura, you're—'

'Listen, can we save this for later?' said Dad quickly, stepping between them, *his* voice hoarse with worry and urgency. 'What's important right now is that we find Laura. I want you to tell us exactly what happened, Sean.'

Sean took a deep breath, then told them how he'd discovered Laura had run away, and what had happened when he'd gone after her, skimming over his close encounters with the caravan and the power cable, concentrating on how he was sure he'd seen Laura reach the main road. Mum and Dad listened to him without interrupting, their expressions a mixture of guilt and worry.

'Right,' said Dad as soon as Sean had finished speaking. 'She can't be far. I'll go and look for her. You two will be safe enough here for the time being. The roof might be gone, but the walls of these old houses are pretty solid.'

'That's as may be,' said Mum, 'but if you think I'm staying here you've got another thing coming. We'll have a lot more chance of finding her if we both search. I can take the main road while you go back up towards Ray's.'

'But what about me?' said Sean. 'She's my sister, and I want to search for her as well. It will be even better if there are three of us looking, won't it?'

'No, Sean, I think we'd rather at least one

of you was safe indoors,' said Dad firmly. Then his expression softened a little, and he smiled at his son. 'Besides, somebody should stay here in case Laura turns up, OK?'

Sean realised there was no arguing with him, and nodded, then watched as they put on their anoraks and checked their torches. 'Don't worry,' said Mum, and kissed him. 'It'll be all right. This storm won't last for ever... We'll find Laura, and I promise we'll sort everything out afterwards. Come on, Phil.'

Dad opened the door to the kitchen and the wind swept in again, bringing with it a salty, wet tang, Sean remembering that big hole in the wall. Mum and Dad pulled up their hoods and went out of the back door and into the garden, Mum signalling for Sean to shut the kitchen door. Sean did as he was told, and stood with his back to it for a second, feeling completely useless.

He was worried for his parents now too, however angry with them he might have felt earlier, and he desperately wished he could think where Laura might be. He started rapidly going over the day's events in his mind, muttering to himself, searching for a clue – the cloakroom, the bus journey, Laura chattering about Thumper... 'That's it!' he suddenly said aloud.

Sean had a good idea of where Laura was. He could almost see her in his mind, running through the mist and down the road to the house, then up the side passage as before, making for the garden shed and the only member of the family who hadn't been horrible to her recently. The more he thought about it, the more certain he was. Laura must be in the shed with her rabbit.

Sean opened the door again, ran across the kitchen, and charged out into the wild night, yelling '*MUM! DAD!*' at the top of his voice, practically screaming it to make his parents hear. They did, and turned to look at him, their faces white in the moonlight, their mouths round 'O's of surprise. But Sean glanced beyond them and saw something that made his blood freeze.

One of the ash trees at the end of the garden was down, the fence and Thumper's hutch smashed beneath its thick trunk. But the other two trees were also being pushed over by the force of the wind, and were obviously on the point of crashing...*onto the shed*. Even as he looked, Sean saw both trees judder and drop a little more, their roots rising from the ground.

Sean didn't stop running, and flew past Mum and Dad. They yelled at him, but he couldn't wait, he had to get to the shed, he had to save his sister. He flung open the shed door, and there was Laura, huddled in a gloomy corner, clutching her fluffy white rabbit tightly. She looked up at Sean, startled.

'Come on, Lol,' Sean yelled. 'You've got to get out of here...*NOW*!'

He grabbed her arm, pulled her outside and ran, dragging her along. There was a splintering noise behind him, followed by a huge *CRASH!*, but Sean didn't look round, not when he felt a *WHOOSH!* of air hit his legs, not when he felt twigs and bits of the shed bounce off his back, not until he knew they were safe, Mum and Dad holding them both, Laura still hugging Thumper.

They stood there for a while, the wind howling, Mum and Dad kissing Sean and Laura and asking them if they were OK, telling them that nothing else mattered, that they were the most important thing in the world...

'More important than the house, the restaurant?' said Sean. And at that moment the wind dipped slightly, almost as if it were holding its breath and waiting for the answer, thought Sean. Or maybe it had just passed its peak.

'No contest,' said Mum, looking into his eyes. 'Cross my heart, OK? If you want proof, I'll hire a bulldozer and flatten the rest of the place myself.'

'That's all right,' said Sean, smiling. 'You don't have to go that far.'

But he felt pretty glad she'd said it, all the same.